LIGHT-YEARS
IN THE
DARK

STORYPOEMS

TODD CRAWSHAW

CrowsnestPublishing.com

Excerpt from
TO THE LIGHTHOUSE
by Virginia Woolf,
copyright 1927 by Harcourt, Inc.
and renewed 1954 by Leonard Woolf,
reprinted by permission of
Houghton Mifflin Harcourt Publishing Company

Various versions of these poems
have previously appeared in
The Author's Mind

Visit: www.toddcrawshaw.com

ISBN-10: 0615381650
ISBN-13: 978-0-615-38165-7

Copyright © 2010 Todd Crawshaw
Published 2011
First Edition

Cover design by Todd Crawshaw
Photo of author by Michael Mustacchi

CrowsnestPublishing.com

Printed in the United States of America

for
those who
inspire

ALSO BY TODD CRAWSHAW

Exploits of the Satyr
a novel

ACKNOWLEDGEMENTS

To Helene, my wife of thirty years, as well to Alexis and Brittany, my daughters, who were essential in making Light-Years in the Dark and my novel, Exploits of the Satyr, possible. Both books were written during the hotbed years of raising a family – a fun, tumultuous, frenetic environment of vigorous growth. How I found the time to create these chimerical offsprings was born from the same questionable stuff of life, a mystery. Neither of these works of art would exist had it not been for them, their love. When I venture off upon these exploratory flights of fiction, they help keep me tethered to reality – providing a lifeline that guides me home (aka the Crowsnest). They are my emotional anchors.

Books are generally written by one person, but the end result is rarely achieved alone. There are many to thank. Some are living, some dead. Foremost, family and friends who (and you know who you are) were willing to read and critique my writing prior to publication.

A special thanks to my editor, Robyn Russell, whose insightful discerning mind and her love of literature has always enriched the end result.

Table of Contents

TABLE OF CONTENTS

*What was the meaning of life? That was all –
a simple question; one that tended to close in
on one with years. The great revelation had
never come. The great revelation perhaps
never did come. Instead there were little
daily miracles, illuminations, matches struck
unexpectedly in the dark; here was one.*

— Virginia Woolf
TO THE LIGHTHOUSE

Through a field of wavering grass came
a procession of men and women. Colors
flowed from their bodies shimmering like
wings of a butterfly skimming over gold
and emerald water. They smiled as they
passed me on their way none would say
to where. Mirrors flashing in their hands
like dangerous jewels in the sun as they
beckoned me to follow but I was blinded
by their swords of light.

I had heard of an enormous garden that was like no other in this world. Once I found it the rumors and fables paled before the truth. The flowers were immense, perfectly formed and brighter than I had imagined. A caretaker dressed in white linen emerged from the foliage to greet me. He stepped with bare feet through the flower beds without harming a petal. He wore spectacles that reflected the sky. His bow to me was respectful, as if to a traveling dignitary, perhaps a king who had ventured far. Yet I felt like a weed.

At a city intersection stood a man who spoke of trumpets in his head, an entire orchestra that performed solely for him. Bloated and shirtless, conducting the air with his hands, he stopped to twirl the ends of his beard before grabbing the torn wings of his coat as if preparing for flight. Passersby paused to take notice of this man who proclaimed he was a conduit, one of sound mind, incapable of resisting the beauty of this nonstop nightmare.

In a remote mountain village lived a man who wore a mask. The residents of this town regarded the new arrival as a pitiful curiosity since it was assumed by all that he was hiding some hideous deformity. He stayed inside his cabin, venturing out only to purchase provisions or for solitary walks at night. The mask covered his entire face, was made of silver, molded to resemble smooth features of a chin, lips, cheeks, nose, and forehead – polished to a reflective sheen. The top and back of his head was concealed by the hood of an oversized leather jacket. He wore hiking boots and baggy jeans and turtleneck sweaters which hid the rest of his skin. When making payments to merchants his hands were mittened, emerging like cautious white mice from his pockets. Seldom did he speak, communicating with gestures. But when he did, his voice was barely audible, thus adding to the mystery. A group of children were the first to challenge him by asking to see his face. He refused with a shake of the head and retreated to his cabin. He evaded the adults too who began enquiring about his circumstances and physicality. This face, like a mirror, became an object of scorn. The stranger was mocked for being aloof, then taunted on Halloween, called names and was known thereafter as the Tin Man. The communal urge to see behind the mask escalated until one day he was stopped in the street by villagers who tore it off. They were more surprised by what they did not find. The man was actually a woman. Her face beautiful – without a trace of any disfigurement. Bewildered by this discovery, several of the men felt compelled to tear off her clothing too. Again, flawlessly beautiful! She screamed and ran to her cabin. The woman was crazy, they assessed. Why else would she disguise herself? Never would they have resorted to such violent action had she conducted herself in a proper forthright manner. Why – and what exactly – *was* she hiding? They demanded answers. They agreed it was their moral duty to confront her with these questions. But she shot herself in the head before they reached her door.

A child with monsters in her head ran screaming across the playground. As her feet left the asphalt touching cool bladed grass her demons transformed into swans and she flew with arms stretched flapping over water to her waiting friends.

What he wanted most was to save lives but in the end he could not even save his own. People arrived with their tattered minds and troubled dreams and he gave them hope. Inspiration found in stories, age-old remedies designed to repair the damage over time. Compassionately he cried, unable to maintain a professional distance. Giving them everything he had – piece after piece of himself until there was nothing left. Like the delicate head of a dandelion blown to bits. Airborne. Adrift. Dismissed. Resigned. Awaiting reassignment. Opening his mouth to be fed. Complying the best he could to comprehend. Sensing in the stories told to him these attendants were his friends.

Three men sat at a table to analytically dissect the reasons for their lives going to hell. After numerous drinks and several helpings of the house specialty of lamb they found many people to recriminate besides themselves. And when asked to leave because of their boisterous conduct they blamed the waiter and unanimously agreed not to leave a tip.

There was a woman who danced herself to death and no one knew why. A crowd gathered to witness her collapse. They stared at her lifeless body until a man dressed in black took it upon himself to bury her. People stood at her grave site confused by the void in their lives left by her absence. In stony silence they came, compelled by gravity. Tossing flowers. Casting judgment. Offering little more than unenlightened commentary on her demise. Untimely. Senseless. A shame. Then a random comment caused frowns: Maybe she was happy?

At the subway station a man was talking
to himself about the inaccuracy of time
relative to his inability to do what he
wanted to do and be where he needed to
be in order to meet his deadlines. He had
overslept. His alarm clock failing once
again to do its job. His office assistants
were failing to assist him too, operating
at a saturnine speed of inefficiency. And
thanks to them he would be unprepared
for an important client who was scheduled
to meet with him in less than an hour.
A meeting which, in all probability, he
would miss—arriving too late. Delayed.
As was the train! What a surprise! With
a sideward glance he informed a woman
standing beside him of this delay, but she
seemed unconcerned, reading her news-
paper, turning a page. Actions meant to
annoy him? Prior to stunning his senses.
Her resemblance to his wife (who had
died prematurely from a genetic heart
defect one year to the day) was alarming.
Nearly stopping *his* heart. He became
lost in thought, recalling how his wife
had kept him waiting. Applying makeup
or sipping her coffee. Before tempering

his impatience with a fey smile and a slow playful pout – getting him to laugh. He detected a gap of missing time. He examined the two large clocks in view. Both facing each other on opposite walls, an institutional monstrosity with bleak hands pointing to roman numerals, the other clock delineating time with graphic strokes of neon to symbolize hour and minute as if from some futuristic diner. The digitized gadgetry on his wrist was equipped with multiple dials and beepers and international times for New York, London, and Hong Kong – confusing him further. He pulled from his coat a hand-held device, poking his digital assistant – confirming he was late, and offering no relief despite its impressive GPS satellite tracking skills linked to atomic clocks precise to within a billionth of a second. He glanced at the woman's arm. Excuse me, he said, Your watch, is it slow? Her lack of response made him wonder if she was deaf or merely rude, so he tapped her shoulder. Excuse me, your watch? Yes? She looked not at him but at the crystal face. He tapped his own, the product of an elite manufacturer who guaranteed its accuracy for years – inquiring: Our times appear to differ. Is yours correct? He was only being polite, having discerned already her watch to be an inferior make, judging by its gaudy design and plastic casing. Yes, she told him. Her tone was unnerving and pragmatic. Said with such conviction. When it was obvious her time conflicted with all the other clocks, he indicated, suggesting she look herself. Instead she spread open her newspaper and continued to read. He bit down upon his lip, flummoxed by her unwillingness to grant a second to see *his* point of view. Perhaps from where she was born (some distant, denser planet, he mused) it was customary to move at slower speeds – minus twenty-one minutes to be precise. Assuming he could trust the precision of time or the reliability of any mechanism to perform accurately. He could not, nor could he trust his senses. This woman's likeness to his late wife was unsettling. Enigmatic. Making him nervous. But why? Reliable sources had informed him women considered him to be attractive.

And he supposed – viewed from a certain angle, if the lighting was right – he *was* attractive. But timing was everything. Curious too. Because if she had *had* the correct time, and he had not been trying to make up for the loss of time, neither of them would be standing at this exact moment in time. He knew the notion to be preposterous the instant he thought it. But were they destined to meet? If so, it was an opportunity rapidly ticking away. Desperately he tried to think of a subject to engage her interest. But only time, its passage, came to mind. Excuse me, he ventured, are you quite certain—But his question was cut off by the blast of a train whistle. He moved aside, allowing her to enter first through the electronic doors. Yes, she replied, turning her head with the hint of a smile. He was drawn to follow and did, seating himself across the aisle from her. When she smiled again with her eyes lingering this time and her lips pursing playfully, he forgot where he was and where it was he had been in such a hurry to be. His heart was pounding audibly and yet soothed by a serenity seen within her eyes as they entered a tunnel together. The wheels clacking over tracks and rocking them melodically back and forth, he could think of only one question to ask. Yes: Is that the only word you know?

The condemned man smoked a cigarette with his executioner and in the short time they had together they had become friends. The subject of blame was not discussed. Neither one held the other responsible. Nor was guilt a commodity they cared to exchange, of little value now, something they both chose to bury. They spoke gravely about the past, the killings they had caused, and wondered how it had changed them. They decided it had prepared them for the moment. An illicit grin escaped from each face as they snubbed out their cigarette and walked away from the mirror in separate directions.

A naked woman was arranging sea shells in the sand. I stopped to ask her what she was doing. Changing, she told me, without looking up. Her hair was long and tangled. In the twilight her skin sparkled with a veneer of salt and silica. Her intricate designs were beautiful but appeared to have no meaning or purpose. About to walk away I stopped, captivated by her eyes opened wide and lips scantly parted as she gazed up to say, We're imperfect creatures, yes? Which is good, no? God would never have allowed us to evolve otherwise to become who we are. My initial feelings to move away or risk becoming enchanted by her madness – seduced by this nymph – had vanished. Inexplicably I found myself on the sand, undressed, lost within her warm body.

On a stretch of desert, for the moment my home, the luminous vision silenced me like a blinding laugh. I knew without asking the answer. It was foretold before I spoke. There was no need to want what I already had. The blossoms of invisible substance took impossible form. I could hold in my hands the petals of regret or let chance flower on the stem. The course of my destiny was already determined by me. The juncture I saw was a reflection of my doubts and as ephemeral as the miracle of water that flowed before my eyes. The beauty was unspeakably real and lost the instant I sought to question its existence.

Survivors of the last war were gathered in a small circle to discuss their luck. Each argued his or her case. Each claimed to be innocent victims of an inevitable systemic breakdown, but bargained for their share of guilt. Each told their side of the story and was accused of lying to the others. Regretting the catastrophe, their common fate, each vowed to never let it happen again. So they drew straws to determine who would die next.

She was known for her collection of unusual things. Wherever she traveled she brought back objects of art to her home. Wood carvings, polished stones, intricate weavings, blown glass, sculpted metals. People said she had an eye for beauty, a gift for finding the truly unique. But she was not interested in what others thought. She collected for herself. Each item represented a desirable moment at some juncture in her life. The arbitrary value people placed on these objects was immaterial with regard to her selection. For example, an expressionistic painting was estimated to be worth millions now that the painter had been discovered by reputable dealers. Whereas a shell found on a beach, collected simply for its rare coloration and shape – costing nothing – was still her most treasured find. She was an old woman by the time her heart faltered and she was placed in a nursing home by her children at the advice of physicians. She felt no bitterness about their decision. Instead, she surprised everyone by voluntarily dispensing all of her collectable wealth. She gave her things to family and friends, donated a few, and then auctioned away the rest. Except for one special gift to herself she kept by her bedside where it could easily be reached. The striations of color were somewhat hazy and the definition of its form not as palpable, yet the memory of a softly lighted beach with her children at play, splashed by blue and salty waves, was very clear. And the tears as they slowly found their way down her cheeks touched her in a way never before felt. There on the sand where she had fallen in love, the place where his ashes had left her hand for the wind, and where, buried in those same infinite granules, she found with a random sweep of her hand a strange and lovely shell. A discovery, made in the midst of laughter, ashes, and tears, when she knew for certain the presence of God.

The creatures of this foreign land were
descendants of god, or so they claimed,
and roamed restless the fertile earth by
concocting mountains of steel and glass,
valleys of cement, and clouds of dust.
From prison towers guarding their spoils
attained from privilege and sacred blood
they perched, vigilant of the thieves who
conspired to pluck out the gold teeth and
false eyes from their ivory heads.

Of little substance, autonomous worlds
of spinning matter interacting within a
predominately empty space is who and
what we are, she said. We were on a blind
date prearranged by friends. It's amazing
we can communicate at all, she quipped,
given the enormous distance between us,
relatively speaking. Dinner was served
and we talked and ate and cogitated upon
the paradox that was us – a network of
molecules and cells amassed in growth to
become self aware yet barely conscious of
our daily involuntary inner workings.
We toasted and laughed at this epiphany.
My wine glass fell with a crash to the
floor as we rose and heads turned but the
galaxy of eyes was beyond our interest.
We left the restaurant to cross a stream
of stopped traffic, idling and gawking, a
gauntlet of headlights glaring at us before
we reached the garden path. An urban
myth, a forest lit by incandescent moons
that transformed us back into children
upon finding a jungle gym and swings
within a clearing. With abandon we rode
the sky seated on pendulums striving for
maximum amplitude and displacement.

Our energetic thrusts ceased once we
glimpsed the glow from a hotel towering
above the foliage, inspiring us with a
notion to wind down in descending arcs,
fingers brushing as we passed.
Grounded, we stood and connected, kiss-
ing walking teetering as we regained our
equilibrium, moving through darkness
into lightness. Bells chiming and doors
opening, we rose inside a mirrored room
of wavering walls, elevated to new
heights. Perched on a balcony overlook-
ing where we had been, she mouthed
something inarticulate while gazing at
the moon. Gazing down into her eyes I
saw stars. And the space between us
closed, inseparable for a time. Our oscil-
lations felt endless because our existence
itself was in question with our bodies
finally coming to rest upon a bed. Our
quest upon waking in the morning was
to recall the past so we could predict the
future emanating from our present confu-
sion.

At the edge of a cliff lived a man who sang praises to the wind. What kept him alive was the desire to reach the ultimate dream of perfection which he hoped he might someday achieve. In a house built of stone and wood he prayed for answers while awaiting guidance in the colors of the sky, the formations of clouds, voices of streams. He lived alone, among the presence of many. Some of whom knew him by name, many names: Son, Brother, Husband, Father, Daddy. As close as they were he heard their voices from far away and faintly rising from the valley, coursing through the trees, ruffling the leaves and feathers of birds, like a wind fluttering softly through the caverns of his heart.

Life's a high-wire act, said a man seated
across the table from me. His eyes were
mesmerizing, intense like a bird of prey.
The trick, he added, is to not look down.
As if calculating our thoughts, he smiled
before confessing, This is not to say I've
never slipped from the proverbial wire.
No! In fact, you might say I'm balanced,
hanging from that wire this very second.
In a grand gesture meant to encompass
his invited guests, the entire house and
beyond, he told us, I can afford none of
this. I owe millions, and yet I am worth
millions! Go figure. Ha! With a flourish
the host summoned a passing servant
hired for the evening to pour more wine,
whose gloved hand shook as he poured,
almost spilling the liquid, which amused
his employer. Why so nervous?
Examine my hands. They were displayed
for us. Steady, you see? Ah, but I sus-
pect you are thinking my *subject* has
good reason to worry, he is afraid of being
fired, and is in desperate need of my
money. Nonsense! Our host surprised
us by standing, then stepping from his
chair onto the table. He raised his glass.

I propose a toast to Fear! Why? Because
without it we are nothing. Fear makes
us who we are. A great adversary who
should be honored. Every waking and
sleeping moment we are transformed and
enthralled by its powers – yet I say, fear
not, or it will possess. To be or not to be
afraid, my friends, *is* the question. To
fear what? Death? A loss of power? A
fall from grace? Nonsense! A world
without fear would not be any paradise!
Can you imagine light void of shadows?
He reached down to grab a wine bottle by
the neck and flung it forcefully overhead.
It turned end over end until it vanished
into the darkness of the cathedral ceiling.
Our host swayed with drunken acrobatic
confidence with a hand raised, poised to
catch the falling object. As his guests –
entranced by his hubris – we were treated
to a raffish split-second wink. The trick,
he proclaimed to our faces voicing alarm,
is to avoid looking down.

Angels are with us, said a woman seated beside me on a plane. I smiled politely and went back to my reading. People often claim not to believe in angels, she went on. What do you think is keeping us from falling from the sky? I shrugged, less of a smile this time, wondering if she might be insane. Outside our windows was a view of storm clouds. Our flight had become bumpy, shaking us about. Followed by shrieks and scattered debris as we plummeted toward our death – as if off a cliff – prior to recovering onto a lower level of air. My hands unclenched. Thank God we were caught. I looked at the woman next to me. She was smiling. We were caught, she repeated. By angels, I suppose. She gave me a sweet smile, pleased by my answer. The turbulence made it impossible to concentrate on my book, and so I shut it. All right, I said, attempting to engage in conversation to amuse her. You convinced me. I believe in angels. I looked up and found myself saying this to an empty seat. Across the aisle a man looked up from his magazine and regarded me suspiciously.

Once, actually several times, I was stranded in a place where people came and went. They never stayed for long. They had schedules. They had arriving and departing flights. They traveled with changes of clothing and currency to exchange. They often appeared lost and tired and in need of direction. They passed the time listening to broadcasted announcements as they watched others, ate snacks, gazed at televisions, read or talked idly, and shopped for souvenirs. They lived in worlds apart, spoke words from languages foreign to each other, and yet they shared a common but transitory purpose — to be somewhere else.

Beside a fire on the beach, under a sky
breaking into colors, we felt and heard the
pounding heartbeat of our ancient home.
Was it fantasy, this ocean within us,
bound by voluptuous skin, as deep and
unfathomable as our desires? Searching
for answers, we explored the catacombs
that hid our dreams. In the depth of
these dark waters we lingered on the
warmth of a sweet salty kiss. And held
our breaths longing for what was beyond
our grasp but gripping each other as if the
sand might wash away beneath us. Then
for an instant – in a light second of bliss
– the shorelines of demarcation lost all
meaning and we danced on the sand like
newborn fish to the rhythm of our
impending birth.

A woman with whom I once shared a
bed asked me if I was prepared for death.
I laughed, then realized she was serious.
She kissed my mouth to silence me and
held me down gently against the sheets.
Her long hair was as soft as feathers and
covered my face. My eyes closing only to
awaken and find she was already in flight.
A bird, but what kind? Her wings cast a
white shadow spreading naked over me.
Her long talons caught my grasping claws
as we conjoined willingly losing our grip.
Succumbing in pleasured disbelief we fell
intertwined flying weightless in the sky,
landing hard, buried deep inside a pillow.
Left breathless, I knew what she'd meant.
We had died together, transported as one.
Combined. Fulfilled. Still, I was wrong.
This was only a rehearsal, she whispered.

What is immortality? asked one angel
of the others fluttering into conundrum.
The question caused a collective silence
that lasted for what seemed an eternity.
In that time the existence of man came
and went, the stars reversed their course,
and once again an infant opened its eyes.
The guardians watched over this delicate
life emerging, so innocent, so vulnerable
to the dangers and infinite possibilities.
Cries from its lungs made them wistful,
praising the consummate miracle of birth.
I have the answer, said one of the angels:
A light in which the stars become you.

She was a woman of incomplete mind.
She formed her thoughts then her words
with deliberate care. The skill of
communicating with a precise formula
of letters and sounds did not come easy.
By the age of thirty-six she had turned
this detriment into an attribute and had
become a talk show host married to her
career, also to a husband, as well as being
a mother of three children, and she still
found time to promote her book, her life
story which was to be made into a movie
once the producers and her agent worked
out the details of price and percentages.
By the age of twenty-seven she had
become a prostitute, and later succumbed
to sleeping in doorways, prior to being
knifed for the worthless possessions she
kept in a shopping bag. She survived this
ordeal only to fight for her life in another
clinic to overcome her years of addiction
to cocaine and heroin. By the age of
eighteen she was a free spirit, abandoning
any hopes her parents had once had of
her achieving a higher education,
quitting college and her music scholarship
to accept a ride from the first car that

stopped to pick her up, two men who drove her to Los Angeles where they raped her and dumped her in front of Universal Studios, a place she mentioned while telling them her dreams of becoming a famous actress, and they laughed, driving off in the rain. By the age of fifteen she was receiving top honors in school, had skipped several grades, had received numerous scholarships to colleges, yet was repeatedly teased by her classmates because of her physical immaturity and her inability to talk without straying to multiple subjects and getting lost while standing up to give a speech. Which was how and why she came to realize, in a haphazard manner, a disability described as a detriment could be overturned into an attribute if a person devoted time and effort to overcoming an inherent flaw. And, vice versa, attributes could become detriments if excelled unchecked, such as a gifted orator lured by words to deceive. Labeled a prodigy by the age of nine she surprised her parents at age six when she climbed onto a piano stool to toy with the keys and her mother walked into the room wondering who it was performing Debussy's *Clair De Lune*. She amazed adults with her comprehension of words and numbers, thus attracting individuals who specialized in these matters to study her mind. She was more fascinated with these specialists than with the problems they presented – calculations leading to infinity, or the many alphabets that made complete symbolic sense, or the melodic vibrations on instruments which produced bursts of applause. And she wished, at times, she could recall then what she had forgotten now so she could inform her live audience and her television viewers by articulating exactly what it was they yearned to know – which would certainly help boost her ratings – if only she could. But she was a woman of incomplete mind.

Each day, despite the weather or his
ailments, he rooted through the hills and
valleys of discarded boxes, dilapidated
furniture, and broken equipment. He
enjoyed the smells, especially latex paint
when it spilled from its container to
waft for a dominant moment over the
pungent odors of rotting food. He was
not overly fond of the swarming insects
that buzzed in competition for their share
of the spoils. But he tolerated them.
They had a right, as did he, to search this
wasteland for treasures no one else
seemed to want. He had found a perfect-
ly good table, the legs rusted and slightly
twisted – adding character to an otherwise
ordinary design – but more importantly,
it was able to stand steady. And over
time he had assembled an eclectic setting
of six chairs. He accumulated toasters,
lamps, blenders, and brought them back
to life. The radios, record players, and
televisions were more difficult to revive,
but he managed to save a few of them.
Computers were an intriguing item he
also liked to tinker with at night, staring
for hours at the intricate maze of their

artificial brains. And from this diligent foraging he had amassed a cozy collection of furnishings for his home, an abandoned woodshed which the owners, whom he had never formerly met, kept threatening to tear down. He slept on a mattress with several broken springs, no complaints from him, the creaking somewhat pleasant. Also there to keep him company was a saxophone missing a few pieces, making music nonetheless, intriguing sounds he enjoyed, learning its quirks as he blew through its tarnished golden body. It was a good life, sorting through the trash for metal, glass, and plastics, along with the resurrected items he sold to repair shops, making enough money to keep him from going hungry. But what he cherished most, aside from his daily work, was the day he had heard the wailing. It was almost mystical – coming from off in the distance, across a desert of debris – a majestic cry for life rising with the sun. A baby, found buried beneath newspapers at the bottom of a cardboard box, placed beside a tangle of wires and piles of dried lawn cuttings. Not in his wildest dreams

had he imagined being so near, and able
to hold, something so beautiful and new.
He could not understand what people
were thinking anymore, to throw away a
living creature. Soon afterwards all the
commotion started, stirred up like a
swarm of hornets seeking him out and
surrounding him with cameras, glaring
lights, microphones, and people telling
him what a hero he was, which meant
next to nothing since it was what any
ordinary human being would have done.
They even laughed at his answer when
he was asked a question by a man in a
suit and tie, a funny outfit for a person to
be wearing in the summer heat while
standing on a sweltering pile of rubbish.
But why mention the obvious? Having
forgotten the question he had to be
reminded and was asked a second time
what it was, exactly, he did for a living.
He thought of the baby and pictured its
cherubic face and smiled at the cameras,
proud to tell them he worked in garbage.

An hour before the gates opened to the public the human couple were locked in their cage between the leopards and the orangutans. Their meals were prepared at scheduled times, served to them on plates, the food consumed while curious onlookers gathered outside their bars. The couple stared back, curious too. As a rule they ignored the questions asked of them, tired of giving the same answers. And the rude comments and gestures became more of an amusement for them as the days went on. To pass the time she read novels and biographies while he amused himself with the remote control, scanning television channels for vicarious thrills in the arenas of sports, news, or simply gazing at the manufactured wonder of nothing in particular. And despite the omnipresence, their awareness of being observed, to celebrate their freedom they talked intimately, kissed and made love upon a bed of sailing sheets to the sound of applause – whether real or imagined.

I was detained and held captive by a man who sought to conquer the world. He had stockpiled an arsenal of weapons dating back to the birth of civilization – Babylonian spears, Roman catapults, Samurai swords, medieval crossbows, grenades, missiles – a virtual museum. These trophies of war were hung from ceilings, displayed in glass cases, mounted on pedestals – dominating each room and hallway with their towering size or their strength in number. I was taken, along with others, to an enormous drawing room walled with tapestries depicting famous battle scenes. Our charming captor encouraged us to pillage with abandon his plentiful liquor supply. He regained our attention by sounding a Chinese gong belonging to a once-powerful dynasty. He unveiled his intent by stating: I am prepared to use whatever means it takes to accomplish my goal. The Caesars and Napoleons had their chance and failed. Now it is my turn. Think of yourself as my honored guest and not as my prisoner. Help yourself to the hors d'oeuvres. I am testing a theory which, in a manner of speaking, you have fallen prey to. It is my belief that unless we are threatened by a force greater than ourselves – such as aliens from another solar system, or from God Himself – we will never abandon our aggressive nature and live harmoniously. Meaning, we are on a path of extinction. Despite our inflated brains and feelings of entitlement, we remain savages. We fear the stranger, his unfamiliar look and his thoughts. In truth, we fear ourselves. Look around at the physical differences. Listen to the cacophony of my words being translated to expose our language barriers. The sound is enough to drive one mad, this babble – is it not? Please, be seated. It makes no difference which chair. Notice the red button. But do not touch it, yet. You sit in an unprecedented position of power that will determine our collective fate. I will explain. The force that is greater than ourselves has arrived. Godlike, but not so alien. You ask, the red button? No, it is a means to an end. Nor should you presume the others in this room are your enemy, all seated in chairs

adorned with colors different from your
own, like a flag representing customs and
traditions of a country foreign to you,
who also find themselves self-appointed,
crowned, upon a throne. By chance? Or
was this preordained? Does it matter?
Yes, yes, I digress. The point is this: One
push on the red button will cause a chain
reaction of atomic explosions that will
annihilate human life on Earth. Think
what this would achieve. No more wars,
no more suffering. World peace! This is
no joke. Unlock the safety. It is located
next to the button on the underside of
your chair. But first, look into the eyes of
the stranger beside you who has the same
decision to make. Realize the threat
they possess is equivalent to your own,
then see them as someone you love – a
mother, father, child, husband, wife.
And apologize to them first before you
put us all to sleep. Now, I bid you good
night and leave you to your own devices.

Chrysalis was the name she bequeathed upon herself, a talented and troubled woman haunted by spirits. She feared their presence and hoped her entourage might provide some security. They accompanied her in limousines, opening doors, carrying bags, and living in her estate. They sat at her long table and dined with her as she ate, which was infrequently, meals requested on a whim. She was cautioned by doctors about her dietary habits and so she compensated by ingesting pills that gave her strength to go on. As hard as she tried she could not resist nor appease the apparitions that materialized in shadows, lingering in the corners of her mind like vestiges from a dream, as silent as her voiceless scream. Mouth parted, she gazed – stupefied by these visitors. Arriving unannounced at her parties, they would appear, mingling among the guests she barely recognized. Overtaken by this influx of spiritual and secular beings, she learned to accept her open mind and overcome her fears. She danced with whomever was bold enough to ask. At the theaters and stadiums she

became possessed of kinetic energy. An
aura of power clearing the way through
the crowd of adoring fans who clung like
trailing particles of a comet, attached and
moving her like the legs of a caterpillar.
Enveloped in a cloudy protective haze,
she arrived transformed on stage, taking
flight – a butterfly, beautifully unaware
of her time on earth.

On route to experience the paranormal,
I walked for days through a downpour of
incessant wind and rain, climbing out of
the storm by traversing the face of a cliff
to its uppermost ridge. I found myself
standing at the rim of a dormant volcano,
an island high above an ocean of clouds.
I was at the cusp of two worlds. Treetops
of the forest from which I had emerged
swayed like soldiers marching en masse
up the slope. Inside the enormous crater
was a frothy lake of whiteness. As a
bird, I imagined diving off the edge into
its center. The crater's transmutable
powers were legendary. The indigenous
tribes who inhabited this mythical region
told of a curse placed upon all recipients
who ventured inside. But being one of
many travelers to this cavity of wonders,
and one practical in matters of the mind,
I descended willingly knowing this vortex
purportedly altered forever anyone who
entered. Becoming deranged ghosts of
their former self – or so the fable went,
told by those who feared to risk taking
the journey themselves. Still undeterred,
harboring the notion I was the captain of

my own vessel, I submerged self-assured
into the vaporous waves. Instinctively I
held my breath as if expecting to swallow
water not air. Breathing relief, I laughed,
and continued to sink. Yet I wondered as
I gazed upwards at the cloudy atmosphere
overtaking me if this desire to look up
was a vestige reflex clinging to my soul.
Was it a primal need to want to see a god
looking down to guide me? Which was
funny. Finding instead the quarter moon
turned on its side in a wide grin, its blind
eye dissolving before me in a wink.

At the time of her conception she was
floating on a ship in the arctic waters.
Her parents had consumed far too much
champagne the night of their fiftieth
anniversary party and they let this tidbit
of information slip out about their
amorous meeting on a cruise to Alaska.
It happened so unexpectedly, innocently,
they pleaded laughingly. They had both
been traveling solo after failed marriages
and had met by chance on the promenade
deck. A premature honeymoon, as it
turned out, since they eloped shortly
thereafter to the surprise of family and
friends. Which was surprising news to
their only child who laughed to hide her
embarrassment upon realizing she had
been conceived out of wedlock. On the
night she heard this story she kept her
husband up late into the morning trying
to comprehend the significance the news
had on her existence. He sighed, urging
her to go to sleep, insisting nothing had
changed, but she would not let the matter
rest. Her mind was flooded with doubts.
Was she a bastard, technically? Or was it
applicable only when the conceiving pair

were unwed at the time of a child's birth?
She didn't know what to tell her children.
Did they need to know? How long before
all her friends and the neighbors knew?
She stayed awake googling for answers on
the Internet while her husband buried his
agitated head beneath the pillows. Which
was when the episode of his near death
experience at the age of seven came up as
a topic. All this talk about preconception
and ocean voyages and her search for the
meaning of life stirred his subconscious,
causing this memory bubble to resurface.
Naturally, she pressed him for details.
He had to ask his parents who lived on
the other side of the continent and who
thought it strange he should be phoning
them at six in the morning (given the
three-hour time zone difference) but were
glad he called nonetheless. They had
almost forgotten the near fatal incident.
Their marital bickering ignited and he
almost hung up on them but he held on
long enough to hear them retell the tale.
He had fallen off an air mattress and,
though he could swim, had sunk to the
bottom of the pool. The verbal assault

resumed between his parents, inflamed
(by a matter of guilt, he suspected) over
the fact neither of them had rescued him.
Truth be told, it was a stranger who dove
in the pool and saved his life. His parents
had arrived at an impasse of silence and
were in need of levity so he pardoned
them and said he loved them regardless
and began to hang up. But at his wife's
insistence he hung on to ask them one
last thing while rolling his eyes at her.
She had to stand and began pacing the
bedroom when he informed her that, yes,
as incredible as it was, the incident *had*
occurred while on a cruise to Alaska and,
assuming the year and month the same,
it was possible – though *improbable* – it
could have been the same ship. She was
compelled to call her parents, who were
not overjoyed to hear from her. Both their
brains suffering from hangovers when she
woke them. Yes, they told her, there had
been a boy who almost drowned. The
recollection produced a belated rush of
giddy laughter from her parents. For this
was how they inadvertently met. Her
father had leapt into the pool, followed by

others, her mother included, and they all
lifted out the boy who they resuscitated.
Later her father had noticed her mother
recuperating under an umbrella, asked if
she would like a drink, which turned into
dinner, dancing and, nine months later,
their daughter. Whose mouth fell open
upon hearing this, was unable to utter a
sound as she clutched the wireless phone
pressed against her head like a magnet,
shocked by the implausible serendipitous
rendezvous which literally caused her to
be, saved her husband to be, and made it
possible for her three children to be too.
She flung the bedroom door open to walk
outside in her nightgown and screamed
as she jumped into their swimming pool.
She was never the same after that. The
network of neural connections threading
her sense of self together had unraveled –
spinning apart at meltdown speed like a
computer shutting off. In the aftermath
she felt dazed. Renewed. Also emphatic
that her family take a cruise to Alaska.
She booked a vacation that corresponded
to the exact month and date she had been
conceived. Their berth was starboard,

near the bow, on the top upper deck –
same location her parents consummated
their love. Her husband worried she had
lost her mind. She insisted she had not.
She held his hand and strolled the decks.
She swam in the pools with her children.
She sipped banana daiquiris and watched
the melting glaciers as they passed. For
she had found peace in these ice walls,
this miraculous waterfall, by accepting
she had no control over the ebb and flow.

For three years he remained her patient, coming to her plush office, lying on her leather couch, and exposing his phobias – fears of acquiring then losing everything he owned. There was much to lose. He had property around the world – estates, vacation homes, villas, even a castle. The numerous companies he presided over made his whereabouts erratic – flying off at unexpected moments to live for weeks in the remote penthouse suite of an exclusive luxurious hotel. Was it any wonder he could not sustain a lasting relationship, he lamented. She consoled him. He became a special case. She worked her psychiatric magic on him until his psyche was restored and she pronounced him cured. He insisted they celebrate over dinner. Since their client-patient relationship had ended, and there was no longer a conflict of interest, she accepted. He wined and dined her for weeks and flew her to a villa in Spain where he proposed his love. She declared hers. They were married in an intimate private wedding. Elated by visions of a bountiful future together, she returned home with her new husband to discover he had nothing – less than nothing. He was in debt to the amount of more than she could fathom. The cataclysmic jolt resulted in a mental breakdown. She lay immobile on his couch (or, in truth, his creditors'), and was unable to rise, pinned down by the crushing weight of her predicament – at risk of losing everything she had worked so hard to achieve. Her husband tried to counsel her, telling her not to worry. She had cured him of these phantasmagorias. They were illusions, the product of mind displaced by matter. Material phenomena lacking spirituality. Deviations disguised as truth. Not real. Not really. Not reality.

She sat in a glass booth selling tickets to
those who wished to view her life. The
price was negotiable but she never gave it
away for free. There was no value to the
encounter if people believed she was
worth nothing. On this philosophy she
built a steady clientele. These patrons
enjoyed her company and left satisfied
when it was time for them to go. She
took pride in the fact that her windows
were kept clean. Some customers hardly
knew what to say, others could not find
enough words to describe what they
thought of her. But it was she who made
it possible for their unbridled passion.
She allowed her body to be their temple
to enter, her mind their confessional, and
her spirit their wandering whore to be
damned and saved.

Lucky was his nickname. Like the scar
on his jaw, both were given to him at the
age of seven by his older brother who
pushed him out their bedroom window.
The three story fall was broken by the
extended arm of an oak tree on which he
bounced before landing in a bed of roses.
Except for the laceration, bruises and
scratches, he was unscathed. He nearly
strangled at birth in the noose of the
umbilical cord and survived fetal distress.
As a child he was afflicted with allergies
and rushed to emergency rooms from bee
stings or from ingesting some taboo food.
So frequent were these mishaps he grew
to admire the local doctors who inspired
him to seek a career in medicine. As a
student he excelled both academically
and athletically, playing football until a
three-hundred pound tackle rammed his
head into a goal post. His helmet saved
his life yet the protective gear could not
prevent the head trauma and subsequent
coma which took him on an out-of-body
flight into a swirling tunnel of fog where
he found himself standing at a lighted
train station. Nothing came to take him

away, so he returned to consciousness, to envision the world anew. Where one day, distracted while snow skiing – the sky exhibiting spectacular purple and yellow clouds – he lost his concentration and his footing on a patch of ice and slid off the face of a cliff. He awoke inside the warm confines of a hospital and body cast and fell in love with a nurse who washed his fallen body most attentively, whom he married, but whose mentally deranged ex-husband shot him as he was running with her hand-in-hand under a shower of rice. Their honeymoon was postponed while he underwent surgery followed by acute rehabilitation so he could adjust to life confined in a wheelchair. The ordeal provided him a greater understanding of the handicapped and a passion to fight for the afflicted. He believed his experience was symbolic of the nation – a powerful body now crippled by senseless neglect, violence and wasteful debt – which became his campaign theme and got him elected to congress where he served three full terms, and in those years co-wrote and helped pass several bills into law.

Lofty efforts aimed to reunify the states,
restoring peace and financial prosperity.
At home his goals were modest – to beget
children and retire from public service to
practice medicine at a clinic. But when
encouraged to run for the highest office,
with the full support of his party, he ran
into a scandal – attacks from his rivals
alleging bribery and corruption, resulting
in a precipitous slip in the polls. Yet,
despite his rebuttals and counter attacks
to defend his good name damaged by the
smear campaigns – refusing to drop from
the race, be defeated by lies, insisting his
innocence – he lost his costly bid for the
Presidency in a landslide defeat. His wife
of twenty years had stood loyally by his
side until the night she was introduced
to a foreign dignitary (at what would be
his last fundraising dinner) who offered
her a taste of royalty and persuaded her,
during the aftermath, to file for divorce.
Jettisoned from both a marriage and a
political career, next his grown children
opting to start families in faraway states,
followed by healthcare reform enacted
into law and spiraling his income into

decline, he felt cast off and anchorless, with nothing left except an abundance of time. So he decided to write a book. The slanderous storms still lashed at him intermittently but never enough to dash his optimism. After his memoir became a bestseller, restoring both his reputation and wealth, he found himself driving on a freeway going nowhere, daydreaming about his strange luck and recalling the telescope of twirling light. Had his mind not drifted towards this colorful world where present, past and future converged, streaming through a collective prism of white, he might have avoided the semi-trailer truck in the oncoming lane which veered over the center divide. Crossing a line that became inconsequential. The sudden impact catapulted him through a shattering darkness filled with crystals. And he knew instantly it was the best possible thing that could have happened.

The interviewer had charmed her with his smile. After being invited into her home, offered coffee, and allowed to have a crew of technicians run cables, cameras, and lights throughout her living room, she soon realized her guest was not only unappreciative but mean-spirited. He sat in her love seat and told her she looked nervous, to relax. The formal exchange began with him quoting praises she had received for her work. Nearly succeeding in vanquishing her guard, he failed, too impatient and inept at camouflaging his attack. Graciously she let his cynicism phrased as questions graze her skin. She deftly avoided any serious damage to her heart by giving him the truth. The rest were deflected answers. She had become calm, more curious as to why her guest was filled with venom. Changing tactics he attempted to cajole his way into her personal life. He wanted to clear up a few unsubstantiated rumors – about an affair with an actor she had never met, an undisclosed settlement awarded to her ex-husband in a lawsuit, her child's autism – and, if all of it true, how was she coping?

She became intrigued by the glimmer of
his green eyes, the fashionably controlled
stripes of his perfectly knotted tie, and
his toupee rising and falling with each
rehearsed frown from his powdered face.
Sweat had escaped through his makeup
and he signaled to have the lights cut off,
abruptly curtailing her answer pertaining
to future plans. He leaned forward in a
gesture to imply they were intimate pals,
and whispered in her ear – commenting
on the silly nature of this show-business
world with its celebrity worship and its
ravenous public appetite that could not
be helped since, he laughed, it kept them
both employed. What surprised her the
most was how much he believed it all –
sounding sincere, deeply caring about the
answer to his final question. Had she
enjoyed being interviewed by him? She
had not, she told him. She had, though,
been charmed by his smile.

Autumn leaves had flamed into colors
when she changed into a squirrel. She
skittered up a tree and chattered at birds.
Racing along a power line she swished
her tail for balance. Clouds, white as
rabbits, chased her from above. She
escaped from the rain inside a treehouse.
She made a nest out of her clothes and
disappeared inside the spotted shell of an
egg and hatched in a lightning flash upon
hearing the thunderous roar of dinosaurs.
In a mirror she saw the rapid expanse of
her head, teeth and eyes – legs aching and
growing horribly too. She clawed and
attacked the tiny creatures – unicorns,
spotted lions, furry dogs, doll-like people.
Flailing them off mountainous bunk-bed
plateaus and table ledges. They toppled
to the valley floor where she kicked and
stomped them with tyrannosaurus feet.
She had become a terror. Frightening her
prehistoric sister who flew screeching
from the room – which signaled the end.
She buried herself in the swamp of her
closet and became extinct. But the grasp
of alien arms transported her back to the
future. Captured, her head examined,

body probed, she was placed in a warm
insulated capsule for further observation.
She was warned to stay still and be quiet,
or receive torture. She awoke hungry.
Her enslavers had deprived her of food.
Cleverly, she pretended to be a good girl
and cleaned up the mess she had made
before venturing down a dark passageway
to sneak into their room. Crawling onto
their large bed, she curled between them,
and became a loving cat.

He was a complex boy. Losing himself in the woods as a child wandering alone. Marveling at the ingenuity of spiders as they secreted tenuous threads from their bodies to orchestrate a symphonic maze. He watched the silk strands pulled taut like strings plucked by virtuoso harpists experimenting for pitch, tone, and tempo. He felt the rhythm of each delicate note upon note, precision woven into a score, composing a pattern of sheer beauty spun into a deadly – yet perfectly tuned – trap. Captivated and inspired, he became a conductor of waves, a man who rode this net of air. Harmonious vibrations at play. Instruments billowing wind. Directing vessels, waving his wand, the keeper of time, attuned to the emotional ties, the catching of flies, the whistling applause.

When a terrorist's bomb blew apart a
national monument scattering to pieces
men, women, and children, it ignited
a worldwide firestorm of condemnation.
The police received an anonymous phone
call from a man who claimed to know
who was responsible: The Scorpion. It
was a moniker invented by the media
which the caller rather liked. As a boy
he played with fire crackers – shoving
them up the rear ends of animals and
lighting the fuses. He was in and out of
reform schools until he became an adult,
was deemed unfit for society and placed
behind prison walls with a life sentence.
He had been convicted of murdering both
his parents in the middle of the night by
soaking their bed sheets with gasoline
and setting them on fire. At the trial he
pleaded innocence through his lawyers
who claimed he was a victim of abuse,
yet in the end even they were secretively
relieved when the judge and jury found
him guilty. After serving less than ten
years, having demonstrated himself to be
a model inmate, he got the attention of a
young attorney who received one of his

letters asking for help. The appeal she filed was granted. Upon researching his case she discovered that evidence had been suppressed – heroin paraphernalia and child pornography found beneath the floorboards in his parent's bedroom. Also prejudicial testimony from a key witness who had been persuaded to embellish the truth. His murder case resurfaced, was broadcasted, generating rallies of protest when a judge overturned the verdict and set him free. His newsworthy status was fleeting – displaced by celebrity worship and the daily rush of competing events – and soon he was forgotten. Years passed before the series of deadly explosions. On a city bus. Inside an airport terminal. At a football stadium. Lives destroyed. And no political faction claiming credit. Only phone calls. Chanting drones and clicks of an insect mocking at the other end – before the receiver slammed down. A fantasy world come to horrid fruition. His nickname would now be a permanent blotch on the annals of history. While tinkering with the makings of a bomb and imagining the destruction of the

world, he blew off both hands and an arm.
Which made him a prime suspect. His
arrest and the disclosure of his past deeds
became fodder for the public consumption
of speculative journalism. Caricatured in
magazines, he was given a devil's red tail.
On the steps of City Hall the surviving
members of his alleged crimes burned
him in effigy before the eyes of cameras.
As he was being wheeled up the steps for
his trial a man broke through the flange of
police protection to deliver a fist into the
side of his head. The spectators cheered.
Slumped in his wheelchair like a doll and
his limbs bandaged stubs, he was barely
cognizant while he sat before the judge.
A broken smile surfaced on his lips when
the prosecuting attorney referred to him
as The Scorpion. His lawyer – defending
him pro-bono and preoccupied with the
money he planned to reap publishing his
memoirs of the ordeal – was proclaiming
his client's innocence and demanding a
mistrial based on the prejudicial nature
surrounding the case. The motion was
swiftly denied. The stern words from the
judge, seated on his throne, had sounded

important, but unheard by the defendant. Whose hearing was impaired by the jolt from his father returning from the dead in the form of another man to box his ear – and getting the last laugh. Yet hearing enough to know they meant to kill him by injecting him with a chemically vile substance, the same way his parents had tied off his veins, cooking up poison in a rusty spoon, inserting a needle. Suddenly a flood of people was parting in front of him like the sea and he was Moses with no arms or hands to block the spit and spray cast upon himself. The commotion stopped by a woman kneeling before him, reaching into her purse for a knife but instead pulling out a handkerchief to wipe his face. He recognized her from an interview on television talking about her only child who was killed in one of the explosions. He remembered all the faces. But this one – so close and searching his eyes – trying to penetrate his mind and see who he truly was – she startled him. How she grasped him around the neck and began to sob. Desperately hugging him as if he was her dead son and it was

the end of the world. And it was, amidst
the lightning flashes firing from cameras,
making him wonder why he had ever
been born. The downpour of tears from
his eyes felt strange, as peculiar as the
warmth leaving his body as the woman
was pulled away. Exchanged by fire, a
burning pain coinciding with a bomb
exploding outside in the streets – a blast
that would vindicate him posthumously
– simultaneous with the bullets that
struck his heart, once, twice, the third
missing his head to penetrate the crowd.
People screaming. The ocean walls falling
down. Drowning them. None of it real.
His confessions to being The Scorpion – a
sordid dream. A cry for revenge. Hatred
channeled into clones of his parents seen
on TV. Wanting but knowing he would
never murder again. Anyone. None of
them. Yet he knew in his heart – like a
lone star rupturing in space – he too was
lost, in some place far from innocence.

She walked into a rainstorm of cobalt
blue. Viridian green. Aquas. Emeralds.
The colors fell around her with each
brush stroke, spattering her clothes, her
hair, the ground. She reached into the sky
and brought down a shower of wetness
with her fingertips. She fell in love with
the droplets as they shimmered, trickling
off dark green branches to brighten a
cluster of mauve and violet flowers.
Within this misty light, along a garden
path layered chocolate brown and zinc
white like icing on a wedding cake, she
was to meet a man at its end. When it
was time she brought his form into being.
With a palette knife she blended dabs of
lamp black and burnt sienna, smoothed it
with sable hairs, then crowned his image
with her fingernail by adding a glint of
gold. She spent the remainder of the day
with him, alone in her studio, his face
staring back from the darkness. By late
evening she knew him completely. He
had emerged from the shadows of her life,
arriving in this downpour of blue to save
her. She washed herself in his presence
with turpentine, then submerged her

body in a hot bath. Up to her neck in a prism of bubbles she dreamed of their life together. She stepped from the water to walk naked across the hardwood floor. She had to see him again. Magnificent, everything she had hoped he would be. She draped her body in a warm towel and prepared a smooth bed of white canvas, stretching and sizing it for the next day. She wanted to be ready. Tomorrow she would paint the sun.

He drove himself too fast. His life was
a blur, punctuated by moments of clarity.
At the altar, his wives, in the honey-
moon suites, the kitchens, bedrooms,
wanting love. His children showing him
a toy, a picture they drew. Road signs.
Looping overpasses. Changing signals.
He felt maligned by the curves, forced to
brake, always something around the bend
to avoid – it never failed. People needing
his advice, his signature on a document.
Meetings that stalled, jerking endlessly
on. An associate asking him: Did he
have time for lunch? His reply: No, there
was barely time in the day to change his
own diapers! Good Lord, he joked, had he
been there *that* long? Obligatory laughter.
The banter of doing business. He would
stand, shake hands, and be first out the
door. From his car phone he conducted
court, instructing others what to do as he
maneuvered the wheel single-handedly.
He reveled in the high speed he traveled.
The perks. Money. The power to veto.
Impulsive desires quenched instantly. Of
course it came with the magnetic draw of
a scrap-metal world envying him. Yet he

was generous. Donations here and there. New homes and pools for his families. His secretaries lavished upon. One too much. Causing a divorce. A marriage. His second, or was that his third? Two more children. Their names temporarily escaped him. He had missed their births. All five of them. Scheduling conflicts. It couldn't be helped. There were many who required his availability. Without his wisdom institutions would fail. The stock market could crash. Nations could collapse! It was like purgatory being sequestered for undetermined lengths of stay, but he would steadfastly remain until the crisis – whatever it was – had been resolved. His opinion on an urgent matter was needed. Would he like his diaper changed? It broke the tension. He expelled a gruff laugh and said—*No.* He would *not!* He would rather have lunch! An advisor came close to whisper in his ear to remind him he already had lunch. He turned his head, a maneuver requiring great effort, to discover who in the blazes was speaking. A nurse!? He noticed the apparatus at his bedside and the many

tubes attached to his body. Shocking
him with a lightning bolt of realization.
He was old, out of commission, barely
functioning. He saw flowers. A basket
of fruit. Greeting cards like over-sized
confetti colorfully implying *Bon Voyage.*
Photographs. Children having grown.
Replacements. Generations emerging.
An emptiness filling the room. Monitors
blipping and beeping cryptic messages to
telepathically inform him of missed
opportunities. As numerous as stars in
space. His wreckage an orbiting trail of
wondrous debris. Compensations.
Constellations. Coughing a last laugh,
he began to lose his signal. His reception
disassembling. Complete static by the
time he reached warp speed. He winked
at the pretty nurse as he slipped away.
Taking with him the comfort in knowing
his body was receiving the best medical
treatment money could buy.

Spitballs hit the blackboard just inches from his head. He whirled around to face his classroom, too late to catch anyone in this mutinous act. It irked him to know he lacked the respect of his students. They made no effort to hide their mirth. Two nights ago he had been held up at gunpoint, robbed of his wallet by youths wearing bandannas to cover their faces. In the parking lot, behind the school, at dusk – they stole his car too, going on a joy ride before abandoning it. Victimized and humiliated, he stood. Had he not been deprived tenure – which would have assured his place of honor as a professor – this indignity never would have occurred. But with the declining interest in higher education, cutbacks, slashed budgets, the prestigious university had dismissed him and reduced him to this trivial pursuit of teaching (no, *attempting* to teach) these pubescent barbarians. He was tempted to select the usual culprits and banish them to the principal's office. But their ranks were growing every day. What was the point? Would they be interested to know that Rome fell in precisely this manner?

From within the city walls, an implosion,
he informed them. Apathy. A divided
populous who lacked interest! A mix of
cultures and racial physiognomies stared
back, as dense as wolves and sheep, all
grinning at him. Perhaps they knew this
and – like the ennui of ancient Rome –
didn't care. He could never reach them.
He instructed them to open their books
and continue with the assigned reading.
A hand shot up. The boy asked if they
would be tested on the material. It made
him sigh. How could he best explain it?
Pacing down the row of seats, he rubbed
the palms of his hands in front of his face
like a praying mantis and dabbled with
the mathematical probability of all their
futures – the high percentage rate of
drop-outs, unwed mothers, incarcerated
criminals, welfare recipients, drug
addicts. He told them, Students, *life* was
a test. They could choose to: 1) simply
exist and accomplish nothing or, 2) apply
rigorous effort in an attempt to improve
their minds...and *still* fail. That was a
hard cold fact. The odds were stacked
against them. So why even bother?

What good did it do to learn that the
innate physical and mental capabilities of
humans had not changed one iota for
about forty thousand years? True. Yet,
how could one explain all these outward
changes – the invention of the wheel
evolving into cars, the harnessing of fire
into rockets and bombs? Should it even
surprise them to know that man's oldest
pastime – congruous with sports – was
warfare? Was that not their goal? The
prizes gained from defeating others?
Capturing wealth and power? He had
their interest now, unstable as it was.
The fate of a Byzantine emperor came to
mind who, in the ninth century, had
been out-witted in battle, captured by a
tribe of marauding heathens who turned
his royal skull into a drinking goblet.
His students were as quiet as a pack of
stalking predators. He tossed them a
meaty free-for-all question: Would they
like to hazard a guess as to what was
considered by many to be the greatest
achievement of the Roman Empire?
Warfare, chariot races, public baths, togas
parties? No—the triumph of peace!

Albeit brief, for a few historic hundred
years or so, a person could travel from
one end of the Mediterranean to the
other without hindrance. His students
were unimpressed. He sat on the edge of
his desk. Suspicious of them all, he
searched their eyes. He risked turning
his back to pick up the chalk. He told
them to imagine themselves as God –
the omnipotent creator and destroyer.
Here it was: Life. He drew a horizontal
white line across the length of the black-
board to represent the span of time life
existed on Earth. Where did man fit in?
He began to erase the line, starting at the
beginning, citing names – protoplasm,
the reign of protozoa, plant formations,
fish, amphibians – ending with the rise
and fall of the dinosaurs and stopping.
He had erased the entire line. He walked
back to face them, holding up the eraser.
What portion did man and woman fit
into this long line of predecessors? With
his fingertip he plucked white lime off
the black felt and displayed it. Roughly,
that much, he informed them. But was
that *all* they were? Insignificant specks

of dust, according to God? Assuming
God exists, challenged a student. Ah, a
show of interest, good! *Assuming*, he
amended. Well? Why should a God – or
anyone for that matter – *care* about mere
specks of dust? To their surprise he
slammed his palm against the eraser and
exploded a plume of particles into the air,
accompanied by his voice to—Wake up!
Sweeping a hand through the dust cloud,
he advised them to start wondering who
and what they were and how they came
to be – for life and death was everywhere.
The atoms that were once an emperor,
once a Brontosaurus, still existed. They
were merely redistributed, passing like
time through their lungs every moment.
Tomorrow would come fast. Soon they
would be dead. And their fleeting speck
of an existence – did it even matter? Yes,
he thought so. Because each of them, no
matter how seemingly insignificant in
this mad teeming world they struggled to
survive within, *mattered*. For they *were*
history. The bell rang, ending his class.
He turned and began erasing the names
of the celebrated figures he had prepared

to lecture about – Constantine the Great,
Julius Caesar, Augustus – achieving fame,
their place in the history books. Why?
Were their lives more worthy of respect?
Did God give a spit more for them than
the condemned gladiator, the unfortunate
galley slave, or his inner-city students?
He listened to the slow stampede of their
feet going out the door – a decibel quieter
than other days, which made him leery.
When he turned around he saw his stolen
wallet and car keys placed on the desk.

She was not to be believed. A beauty
undefined. Amorphous warmth entering
her body like a lover. Fulfilling her
desire by not wanting, simply accepting.
His voice a whisper echoing deep within.
Melding them as one. He was what she
wanted to be. An ecstacy. A conception.
Of perfection. Awakening. She awoke.
He was nowhere. Lingering everywhere.
A vapor trail. Soft as morning light.
Impressionistic. A destination to share.
She lay sprawled in the folds of bedding.
The sky parting. A new sun being born.
Waiting to give birth. Gazing as a child.

On the outskirts of a small town miles from the nearest city lived the two-headed man. A freak of nature. In reality, twins sharing organs and extremities. Whose parents were flying trapeze artists, hired by a circus primarily to acquire their son. Lacking talent, they fell to their deaths when he was only a child. Adopted by a family of clowns he traveled like a gypsy for two decades, enduring ridicule and visual scrutiny day after day, until finally he had had enough. He married the bearded lady and they left show business to hide, also to seek out a semi-normal life. Their first child, a son, stopped growing after the third year and remained a midget but developed a talent for jumping onto their Great Dane and riding it bareback. Their daughter was wild and ran with a pack of unruly boys who taught her how to swallow swords and juggle knives. Their baby boy had a shy disposition and kept to himself but grew into a giant who could barely fit through the doorways of their home. Other families might have cursed their fate, believing their lives to be cruel jokes created for the amusement

of a demented maker. But they were not
like other families and were thankful to
have found a place where people accepted
them. Isolated by distance, they became
close friends with their few surrounding
neighbors. There was the woman with
purple hair who talked in tongues, a man
who lived in a tree and squawked like a
crow, and the albino triplets who sang
songs in a haunting three-part harmony.
There was also the blind three-legged
stub-tailed dog who found shelter in their
yard. A cozy world that would change.
It happened the day a caravan of trucks
got lost and wandered into their out-of-
the-way town to stay the night. His wife
by then had discovered electrolysis and
fashion magazines and makeup and acted
hysterical and put on a good show –
refusing to comprehend the wiles of her
children. As a parent, he too felt the
pain, the loss, and fear for their safety.
But being of two minds he understood
their desire to want to leave home and
experience the circus for themselves.

It was love at first sight for him. For her she had to get used to his face. He looked like her Yorkshire Terrier. It was his red shaggy beard and eyebrows. What she was attracted to was his eyes – dark and gentle, with a sparkle to them – again, like her dog's. He came into her pastry shop early each morning to buy something sweet. He ate it while sipping coffee and they chatted about nothing in particular – the weather, town gossip, news from the lives of their children. It was a pleasure for him to watch her greet the customers whom, he suspected, came in to see her more than for her selection of delicious treats. She was stylish in her colorful aprons, often adorning herself by wearing hats with the plumes of a bird shooting skyward and dancing lightly above her in the air. He had an antique store down the street which he opened for business an hour later. Because he was in love with her, secretly of course, with both of them recently widowed – coming up on a year for her, three years having passed for him – he bought a blue and yellow parakeet that reminded him of her. He named the bird Sugar and gave her a home within a domed wrought-iron cage that he had in his shop. It was more than one hundred years old, ornate with floral designs and painted white. He carried the parakeet with him to and from work and Sugar became a regular customer in the pastry shop at daybreak. While Sugar pecked at the crumbs of donuts and jelly-filled croissants, the two of them chirped like birds themselves. They taught her to sit on their fingers and, over time, got her to say things. First: Hello, Sugar. Then: Good morning. Next: Something sweet? And after weeks of practice: I love you. Customers gathered around to listen, to voice their delight, the doorbells tingling as they came and went. Since her store had more traffic than his, and since the parakeet loved the attention, he gave her Sugar as a gift, telling her it was an early Christmas present. She almost cried, accepting his gift on a promise from him that he would continue visiting her in the morning. Additionally, he would come to her house for dinner. He arrived punctually, holding a cluster of Iceland

poppies from his greenhouse. She made a
place for them in a vase at the center of
her dining room table. Waiting in the
living room, he listened as she sang in
the kitchen, Sugar singing on a nearby
perch, and he became intrigued by a
shaggy face staring up at him. There was
something familiar about the dog. Its
mouth opened in a panting smile, a pink
tongue displayed, licking his offered hand.
He stroked its silky fur and this seemed
to calm them both. The evening chill of
an approaching snowfall clung to his skin
but he was warming nicely beside the
fire she had made. The glowing embers
and orange flames swayed hypnotically.
From another room he heard her voice
call to him, in a playful trill, announcing
dinner. Her love for him was spoken.
He turned to look at Sugar chirping on
her perch, bobbing her blue and yellow
head. He felt the warm kiss on his hand,
a nuzzling head against his arm. And at
long last his frozen doubts melted. He
recognized himself in her dog's eyes and
realized he was home.

He raped his wife then kissed her crying face before collapsing into sleep. Later that night he was handcuffed and shoved into the caged backseat of a car with flashing red lights. Driven downtown past decaying office buildings and abandoned warehouses he descended with the vehicle into a mausoleum-shaped structure down a cement ramp to a cavernous garage. He was ushered through a maze of elevators and passageways. He heard gears turning and cables creaking that reverberated into hollow depths from behind the walls. Fluorescent lights buzzed and flickered to indicate a power source on the verge of collapse. Inside a windowless room with off-white walls discolored like a bruise and stains oozing out from its corners, he was told to confess. He refused, claiming he had committed no crime. They slapped his face and laughed. Was he a gambling man? Did he like playing poker? They pummeled him with more questions that made no sense. He was told to sit, which he did, around a small table. They offered him a beer which he declined, then he changed his mind and took it, thinking…What the Hell. He flinched when struck on the back with a flat-handed slap as if he was their buddy, an old chap, a good sport. Five-card stud. An equal opportunity game, they jested. Stacks of red, white, and blue chips were divided among the players. Gratis. But after that, the bets got personal. They let him cut the cards. His hands trembled. He tried to enjoy himself, had a second beer, even smiled as he began winning. But his luck changed. He lost everything he had. The cash in his wallet. Three credit cards. His wrist watch. Wedding ring. Next his clothing. He sat naked in a cold metal chair with the policewomen snickering and pointing at his shriveled manhood as they proceeded to win his car, his house, and his dignity. He signed documents stating they now owned him. They gave him back his clothing and said he was free to go but if he was not a good little boy they would return and punish him severely, next time. The sunrise racket of their fading laughter humiliated his hungover mind as he hurried to catch a bus. At work he could barely function.

He punched the cash register and had a
vehement distrust for the computer as it
tracked the barcodes. He apologized to
customers when caught overcharging
them, triggering his anger to berate his
subservients for bagging the groceries too
slow. When he arrived home that evening
he wanted to ignore his wife and watch
football but she confronted him with her
sad face. He told her to forget last night.
It was a mistake! Like his whole life! –
he yelled at her – a god-damned mistake!
She agreed but wanted him to apologize.
He slapped her. Immediately regretting
it, he apologized. He left the house to
get cigarettes and brought home flowers.
She thanked him with a kiss and a hug
and a plea for him to seek help from a
higher power. He hated how she shoved
religion in his face. His annoyance with
her festered into an urge for sex as they
climbed into bed. So he clutched his wife
between her legs with a thought that by
reinforcing his matrimonial rights would
provide a lift. But he was too tired to get
aroused. And her moans were not utters
of pleasure but murmured prayers like a

voodoo curse and they killed any chance
of stimulating his flaccid libido. So he
removed his middle finger from inside her.
Desperate for sleep but fearing to let go,
the loss of control, and the police coming
to arrest him, he felt the muzzle of a gun
pressed to his head as he awoke with a
flashlight on his face. His wife sleeping
peacefully as he was led outside in his
pajamas. They drove him to the end of a
dirt road far from the city. As the car
came to a stop it occurred to him that his
abductors were not the police. Hovering
far off in a grove of trees was a spaceship.
Their words turned into alien gibberish.
He was escorted under an enormous disc
and beamed aboard. Although terrified he
found the encounter not that unpleasant.
He was transported through passageways
resembling fiber-optic tubes reducing
him in size before probed and examined.
The temperature was warm, a soothing
bath that circulated around him and he
surrendered to the loss of equilibrium
and became docile, placed on a conveyor
belt which delivered him to a domed
room with walls illuminated to simulate

a blue sky. He floated over churning red liquid past rows of humanoid creatures standing above him on each side. All hovering in semi-transparent uniforms, their sexual identity was clearly exposed. All were female. He smiled. They did not. Their apparent leader was seated on a high platform resembling clouds and ignored his arrival. Head turned away, she was examining a wall of cryptic blips and messages beyond his comprehension. Swiveling around, she faced him holding a glowing scepter resembling a cattle prod. She did not look pleased. Nor was he – upon realizing this woman was his wife! His alarm was expressed in a whimpering submission as the lights and power from this mother ship died – gone in a flash. He bolted upright, in a cold sweat, his eyes opened wide. His heart pounding. He turned and saw two eyes glowing in the darkness. Was he still dreaming? The voice he heard was strange and yet so familiar it sent a shock wave to his organs – to his groin. Go back to sleep, she said. Without hesitation, he obeyed.

She was searching for the essence of her self. In the books she read. In the people she met. The men she loved. The work she created. She wanted the stories to be real. Each mind to be interesting. The effort to be worthwhile. The trust to be reciprocal. Yet she revealed herself too soon. Exposing her world for the masses to touch. Blind devotion leading them down her pages. Braille-moving fingers fondling her body of work. Devouring her like a delicious novel. The romances sweet but tawdry. The people becoming fictional. The dialogue sounding false. An over-used line, again. The climaxes anticipated. An unsavory end. But a desire for more. Someone better. It was her essence. This search to live.

Locked in his private hell at the end of
the hall, in an ordinary room, was a man
held hostage by himself. He had a gun
aimed at his head. His demands could
not be met and he wanted to die. He had
no illusions about God or what to expect.
Nothingness. An infinite non-existence.
The so-called Supreme Being was nothing
more than a fabrication inside the mind,
implanted there by deluded ancestors.
Propaganda passed on through the ages.
This notion of an omniscient god was no
more than what a night-light served for
children, a lie that reassured – like Santa
Claus or the Easter Bunny – providing
false hope. The lapse in his will to pull
the trigger was only the body's innate
mechanism for self-preservation, not the
result of any superstitious fear. And the
paranoia? This strange sensation urging
him to think he was not alone. It was a
biochemical trick! An elaborate illusion.
Something he knew quite well – knowing
how to recognize the signs. Magic being
his forté. The way he dazzled audiences
night after night by walking on water,
being murdered and coming back to life,

among other tricks. As a magician he
admired all the great ones from Houdini
to Christ. He had won contests and
awards as a child from his sleight-of-hand
manipulations – making coins disappear
and doves emerge as if out of nowhere.
Achievements that meant little until he
mastered the ability to escape imminent
death – locked in cages sunk underwater
or trapped in boxes pierced by swords.
Only then did he begin to believe in his
own powers. Elevating his game to a
new level. He invented a guillotine that
lopped him off at the neck. Guided by a
voice from this severed head, his body
groped blindly until reattaching itself.
He performed inside stadiums filled to
capacity, deceiving the masses into
believing they witnessed an airplane full
of passengers explode, vanish – reappear.
Critics could find no flaws. Nor could
the naysayers who plotted to expose his
illusions and discredit him. Proclaimed a
genius, he wandered the hotel lobbies
and streets late into the night, unable to
rest or find peace and concluding that life
was no longer preferable to death.

Beneath the intricate layers of deception he had devised – polished to a spectacular sheen – he knew he was nothing more than an exceptionally gifted fraud. The need to beguile others into believing he possessed extraordinary powers had once been gratifying and provided some solace. But the public's expectations and demand for grander thrills grew to be excruciating – a burden as palpable as a lead weight. What began as a boy's fanciful hobby, an amusing diversion turned career, changed into a dangerous obsession and relentless pursuit to invent near-impossible stunts. A chronic manic challenging of the mind to discover another miraculous creation, like finding a rare diamond only he could bring to light. The reward was euphoria. The dullest environments became bright, the people interesting and the air worth breathing. In the aftermath, a collapse, a requirement of rest in which he suffered the miasma of doubt and self-loathing. He sank into a listless bog of drowning depression. Voices mocked and jeered. Artfully disguised to sound like his ex-wife or one of his many fired assistants, or a member of his estranged family. All of whom he had made disappear from his life. But being a devout pragmatist he refused to heed the call of these avenging furies and seductive sirens who sought to lure him to madness with songs crashing upon rocks that shored disastrous truth. Still these phantoms proved difficult to remove, more than straight-jackets, locks and chains, or the nailed confines of an interred coffin. He held firm, his finger crooked on the trigger, refusing to heed or concede to delusions, yet he confessed: No, he was not a pleasant man! Neither had his father nor had his mother been. Whatever he did was never quite right or enough to please them. Not once had he received their praise without a disclaimer attached. Cheap with kindness, the way they were with money – hoarding and withholding. His revenge? Forcing them to admit (if only by proxy) that he was more gifted than they would ever be. Love, like God, had a place in his heart. Both displayed as plastic trinkets. The four-letter word hanging from a rearview mirror. And the crux of a plastic Jesus was stuck to his limousine dashboard. Rarely did his passengers appreciate the sardonic humor. Not even the woman he married, after vowing to love him, whose sincerity he doubted – and, true to form, divorcing him, not even wanting his money, proving in a perverse way maybe she had loved him. Which left only his employees, whom he demanded nothing less than perfection – an imperative or the illusions would fail.

Therefore he was monetarily generous to vouchsafe his career. His infamous temper was to be accepted as part of the job description (although unwritten) if his assistants wished to collect their inflated paychecks and fat bonuses. But still, the want was endless. Everyone demanded something he was unwilling to give. Unlike his cat, with fur the color of mercury, tolerating him, and he tolerant of her. Not so with his sister and brother who joked at the last family gathering by comparing him to Doctor Frankenstein with lightning bolts and his monster – a mad scientist! Dismissing his career as a freak show. Their laughter was like a cascade of bees buzzing and swarming inside his brain, to sting havoc, to taunt him to pull down on the god-damned trigger. Tears were squeezed from his eyes, squinting as he unlocked the void by pressing the latch. His only prayer – for this agony to end. The gun exploding. His head shattering to pieces. Shards of a mirror collapsing and scattering across the floor. Stunned, he stared. At a bullet hole in the wall. All the crazed voices sucked inside. The pain of locks and chains vanishing too. He pushed at the chunks of glass with his shoe, examining the pieces, as if clues to a puzzle. Once convinced he was alive and not dead, he laughed, acknowledging the fact. In appreciation of the magic. Even smiling, not even wanting to know how the illu-sion worked. To know would nullify the trick. But he knew, beyond a skeptic's doubt, he had escaped death not on his own. He had received help from an anonymous assistant.

From pop-up books to electric trains to video games, he dismantled all his toys. Within days after flirting with the notion of play, he divided each item, strewn in pieces across the floor, decomposed to nuts, screws, and micro chips. Neither his father nor mother could comprehend their son's destructive nature. As he grew, he advanced from disassembling wind-up toys and play stations to taking apart toasters, cell phones, televisions. Hard-earned money gone straight down the drain, his father complained. Poured next into child therapists, all hired and willing to listen – for a price! Specialists who determined their son to be retarded, exonerating them of any parental blame. But then a motorized lawn mower got dismantled down to its rotor blades and spark plugs and his father lost control – slamming a fist through a sheet-rocked wall, and inadvertently lashing his wife in the face during his unrestrained rage. A leather belt accidentally cutting her lip while he whipped their son incessantly before she intervened. Pleading defense on her son's behalf, his innocence, since he never harmed a living soul, was never cruel to animals, and was a loving boy. Whom she loved, but did not fully trust, and so she hid her treasured items behind padlocked doors and bank vaults for safe-keeping to guard them against her son's inexplicable temptations to deconstruct. Though not on a daily basis, this desire to destroy inanimate objects. Weeks and months would pass before an appliance fell victim to his malicious curiosity. If *only*, his father lamented, he learned to put the damned things back together! Which was the approach his parents took from the advice of pediatric clinicians and counselors, who encouraged him to pursue this constructive path, until it became clear this boy had no interest in resurrecting anything, only in knowing how these mechanical and electrical devices came apart. Following puberty, he discovered girls and his parents were thrilled and relieved, since his obsession to dismantle stopped. So they thought. They purchased athletic items – footballs and mitts – to encourage an energetic interest in sports. He played hard and received top honors, winning the hearts and minds of many, especially members of the opposite sex. At age sixteen he was surprised by his parents presenting him with a car to celebrate his maturity, this milestone, his ability to drive legally and be semi-independent, but secretly they worried he would fall prey to his old habits and take the engine apart. Which was not uncommon among teenage boys. But misplaced were their worries. Their son's interest in dismantling things had shifted to unhooking bras in the comfy quarters of his automobile and single-handedly stripping the panties off dates. His fingers being nimble, having years of experience, he quickly determined how things fit and came off. After a series of maneuvers, knowing where to touch, what buttons to push, women went to pieces, melted, virtually coming undone. He credited his childhood predilections for this prowess to attract, arouse, then unloosen girls who were very complex, wired differently, requiring much more work than toys, turntables or any video game. Yet receptive, females delighting in his abilities. Not so much the parents, nor the school principal, who were all ineffective at chastising and belittling his achievements, his extracurricular activity, determining the behavior bad, warranting detention, plus a one-week suspension. During the break he broke into the office of administration late one night to unlock and erase the computer banks of memory. Resulting in his expulsion from school. Deemed a troubled youth and in need of discipline, he was sent off to a military academy by his parents. Which led to the Army and training for war. Placed on the battlefield to perform in a special squad. Facing fear and swathed in protective gear he dissected volatile mechanisms. His survival skills challenged daily with each time-sensitive device constructed with the sole purpose to obliterate life. Defanging venomous snakes he equated his mission to a song, singing "Another One Bites the Dust." Joking to ease the tension among his cohorts who never mentioned the countless lives they saved. Yet keeping score. An unofficial game they played. An intrepid bunch of risk-

takers functioning as one, not disengaged.
Each a vital component, an integral part,
holding the universe together, was what
he felt but would never say. As with love
– a commitment at the core of existence –
he was hell-bent and heaven-sent to save
this fragile place, he had come to believe.
Until one day a split second too late he
too was returned to his elemental parts –
into particles as nebulous yet as pure as
the medal of honor his parents received.

The poet had gone insane. Ingesting a
chemical substance believed by pundits
of religious esoterica to be the forbidden
route to God. Discovered near a dead sea
were scrolls of his work written under
the influence with his senses heightened
and deranged, was how they came to be.
Found in a vision – picture this – an old
woman with a pretty face and a mean
laugh standing at the ends of the earth.
The oceans all dried-up. No more tears.
Lost souls offered to the highest bidders.
Worthless gold thrown madly at her out
of fear. Bargaining for salvation as others
tried to solve times tired equations and
overturn the weeded garden into flowers.
Again, what was the question, or reason,
why this man had scrawled to be heard?
Enraptured in fruitless prophesy. Fingers
scribbling blood marks into sand script.
Was it a curse, this punishment of words?
Pronouncements of the unforeseeable to
be foreseen as tragically incomprehensible
and disbelieved. No need then to heed
warnings if truth appeared wrong when
right. Alas, for naught was his sacrifice
in gaining this powerless insight.

She might just as well have been her cat chasing after a reflection of light dancing across the wall. The mercurial vision of who she was kept eluding her. In a flash traveling backwards she glimpsed herself timeless as a child. On the surface of the mirror she saw her renewed face. The bandages removed, the once bruised and swollen flesh smooth, wrinkles tapered, turned back like clockwork. An appeal she hoped to gain along with her husband lost to his preoccupations, still desiring to be perceived as a lion. It had long been a source of pride, for him, as well for her, rewarding themselves with the bounty of his spoils. But growing old took strength and his mane receded with time. Now when he roared it accomplished nothing except to threaten the love they had both fought to maintain. Once aggressive and confident in their union, their bodies sleek and tan, the envy of the savannah, they now sat apart, no longer the animals they had been. But their passion for life had conceived, nurtured and raised offspring. Existence affirming itself. Procreation come and gone. The spectacular dust settling around them. But the questions remained. Was it ability or stupidity to have chased after the sun? Good fortune or deception to have caught it? Acumen or folly to have sold it? She watched as her husband dangled his gold watch from its chain, toying and teasing their pet. They exchanged smiles. A moment for reflection. Metallic glimmers projected upon a living room wall – with their cat pouncing after it. This pursuit of light.

She was a child not a pet, and a girl not
a toy, but his tormenting bordered on
cruelty only man knew how to inflict on
another. They first met as children. He
pulled her ponytails. He made her laugh
until she cried. He called her brain dead,
vegetable head, along with all the other
names of wit that hit school walls and
stuck. She told her dog about her friend
and how one day they would be married.
He took her into the woods to play with
her mind, then her body, examining it
before exhibiting and imposing his own.
Overpowering her like a tree rooting into
earth, or a rockslide, as unpredictable as
she was, a warm torrent coursing through
his limbs, splashing clouds into the sky.
Around others he teased and avoided her.
He was heartless when he was not alone
with her. Always restless like an animal,
wanting the ravage speed of a cheetah or
the flight of a hawk. He shot past her –
roaring off on his two-wheeled machine.
She never understood where he was going
or why so fast, or why her body changed
and swelled, pounding like ocean waves.
Her stomach a whitecap cresting toward

the sun. Flowers rising from meadows.
Babies born. Wings fluttering into air. A
dream of birds soaring through her lungs
as she sang a song of lullabies. Waiting,
never doubting, one day he would return.
But the vacant look in his eyes was new.
Alive but asleep, inside a bandaged head,
far away inside his mind, said the doctor.
She imagined the crash of a wave hitting
sand petals crushed hard into dirt broken
apart like the bright red machine he rode.
The streets flooding and riverbanks over-
flowing with tears before it would end.
The sun, she believed, would come again,
bringing colors to guide him through the
dark pavement wall he struck to find his
way home into her heart. Looking lost
when he arrived, his eyes searching for a
smile that she alone was there to give.
She cradled his body to reassure him –
his tentative light. An awakening child,
delicate as a flame. He was going live,
not as before. Reborn her equal. Slow in
mind but not lacking of love. Knowing
her now completely, he no longer wished
to grow wings and fly away.

He fought to climb the ice walls into
darkness and touch the stars. He fell back,
hands burned, eyes blinded, and cried —
Why? The crowd rejoiced at his success.
No, a failure, he insisted, but was denied.

She was falling to her death like the earth into the sun, slowly and relative to nothing that mattered anymore. So she accepted the stranger's offer to buy her a drink without bothering to turn and see who this new Patron Saint of Alcohol was. The offer had been conveyed to her by the bartender in a language of gestures she understood. A Bloody Mary was placed next to the half-emptied one in her hand and she closed her eyes. She caressed the darkness and felt the presence of a man taking the seat beside her at the bar. She turned to see who it was – and saw the penetrating eyes, the long hair, beard, and gaunt face. She blinked and exclaimed – *Jesus* – to herself with a laugh. The man toasted her with his drink. A Screw Driver. Apparently the favored breakfast cocktail of our *Lord*, she assessed with a clink of her glass to his. Her easygoing smile and beauty, albeit fading, concealed a cynicism coupled with a shrewdness for discerning another rejection forthcoming. It would come, as always, with a naked expression of surprise at her ugly croak of a voice and the realization she was a deaf

mute. She had calloused herself to the
unavoidable grimaces, the blatant looks
of disgust, and even the pitiful smiles
from the well-intentioned hapless souls.
She decided to be coy and deceive her
current suitor, at least for one more free
drink. He was inquiring about her name.
She dipped a finger into her drink, raised
it to her lips and sucked it seductively.
She challenged him with a quizzical gaze.
Someone had placed coins in a jukebox
and vibrations were pumping the room.
Mary, he guessed, as in Magdalene? She
applauded him softly with the rehearsed
act of a consummate mime. He pointed
to himself, indicating it was her turn.
She spread her arms to form a crucifixion,
her head slumped sideways, mocking his
resemblance to the renowned savior. He
laughed and nodded sheepishly – as if to
lie was inconceivable – and bowed his
head humbly. He was now playing mind
games with her. She dropped her arms
and narrowed her eyes, playfully drunk,
amused by her opponent. She signaled
like a traffic cop with her hand for him
to stop and wait while she dumped the

contents of her purse onto the counter.
She found her driver's license, indicating
the photograph as proof of her identity,
tapping a fingernail on the name typed
beside it. Smiling triumphantly, she
chalked a point for herself on an invisible
scoreboard. She took a sip of her drink
and gestured for him to produce the same
credentials. He emptied the items from
his pockets – some coins, crumpled bills,
and a few ordinary rocks. He clutched
an imaginary steering wheel, rotated it
wildly, then shrugged. He did not drive.
But, as if to provide alternative proof of
his identity, he took a coin off the bar.
With a theatrical flourish – palm closing
then opening – he transformed the silver
into a gold ring held between his fingers.
She yawned, unimpressed. He waved the
bartender over, asking for a glass of water
in a wine glass. She frowned and glanced
at the distracting shaft of light pouring in
from the open doorway. Hovering there
like an alien beaming down to Earth and
trying to take form. Dust motes were
swirling hypnotically in the radiant glow.
She had to readjust her vision to the dark

confines of the saloon. Late morning and the place was empty except for the two of them and the regular drunks she knew. She pursed her lips and returned to where she was – as if in the middle of a chess match and not willing to be outdone by some gypsy charlatan. Which was what she surmised him to be. She narrowed her eyes and made a cross with her index fingers as a curt denouncement about matters of the heart, Heaven and Hell, God and the Devil—and him! Angry at his parody. His offering her the ring as though proposing marriage and playing the groom. She suspected some jokester in the bar had orchestrated this sick joke. She offered back her middle finger and rose to leave but was stopped by his hand placed upon hers. She was overtaken by a jolt of warmth that gushed through her body. The sensation caused her to gasp. No one had touched her like that before, not since her father or mother, not since she was a child. The sky was in his eyes, this unwavering unfathomable blue. She let her fingers be kissed, transforming her into something strange and beautiful.

She was clearly under his spell, drawn to the power of his gentle smile, his eyes leading hers to focus on his hand held before her face, to an open palm, into its center. The instant she realized what he was showing her – a blood-stained scar, the circumference of a spike – he tapped her forehead with a force that knocked her off the barstool. She heard laughter as she came to her senses. She rose off the floor screaming. But he was gone. Everyone in the room was staring at her. The shaft of light was receding from the doorway. She then realized what it was, what it was that had happened. She was hearing the sound of her own voice, and she fell to her knees and wept.

His body displaced the air as he walked
along a sunlit path and questioned the
worth of his existence. What if anything
would he leave behind? He beheaded a
flower to examine its ephemeral beauty
and purpose, sniffing then twirling it by
the stem, before tossing it back to earth.
As all things return again and must end.
Walking stick clicking, he mused, *Amen.*
A life undone to become at best, what?
A pleasurable scent or melody to linger,
to enlighten the mind lost in reverie, to
excite the puzzled facets of one's day?
He imagined his grown children pausing
to smile, their senses stirred by a mental
drifting remnant arabesque to exclaim:
Yes...*that* was who he was...or who he
wanted to be, loving to delight, because
he saw both sides, wanting all to agree.
Yet raging at complacency and himself,
his worst critic, striving for heaven in
this often living hell. So why go gently?
Succumb and fade, be tossed away or –
worse than be forgotten – be remembered
as some scuff of a troubled foot scraping
unmolded clay.

In the vast shadow of a garden he was on
his back questioning the moon and stars.
It took more than the strategic leap of an
astronaut's faith to reach the blackness.
The luminous net of clouds would be too
soft and forgiving to stop or catch his fall.
He had to first escape the wrenching grip
of his body – arms, legs, head – restrained
by the centrifugal swirls and tug of the
cosmic whirlpool. His standing was an
effort requiring will, an acquired skill, to
artfully command the sailing winds with
his passionate hands. Head spinning like
carnival wisps of cotton candy lifting off
to be whipped and reformed into orbit.
Fingers extended, probing space, tendrils
snaking through the tall grass rooted in
cold sand. His clenched memory eroding
into bits and slipping away in fistfuls.
He shut his eyes with the thought to
never wake but awoke to a passing light
– a light he had come to be.

The river asked me who I was to be gazing so longingly into her curving body of cascading dreams and shifting beauty.

"Good fiction sets off a vivid and continuous dream."
John Gardner (On Becoming a Novelist, 1983)

"I meant to write about death, only life came breaking in
as usual." Virginia Woolf (Diary, 1922)

"To write the text you have to live in the myth of it."
John Fowles (An Interview with John Fowles by CM Barnum
- 2009 Project MUSE Journals MFS Modern Fiction Studies)

"Writing is a socially acceptable form of schizophrenia."
E. L. Doctorow (Interview in Writers at Work, 1988)

"The sole purpose of human existence is to kindle a light
in the darkness of mere being." Carl Jung (Memories,
Dreams, Reflections, 1962)

"Exaggerate the essential, leave the obvious vague."
Vincent Van Gogh (Letter to Theo van Gogh, 1888 in Arles)

"Heaven is spread out across the earth, only people
don't see it." Jesus Christ (Gnostic Gospel of Thomas: 113)

"Writing is utter solitude, the descent into the cold abyss of
oneself." Franz Kafka (Letter to fiancée, Felice Bauer, 1913)

"Out on the edge you see all kinds of things you can't see
from the center." Kurt Vonnegut (Piano Player, 1952)

"I saw the angel in the marble and carved until I set him
free." Michelangelo (Letter to Benedetto Varchi, 1547?)

"There is absolutely no point in sitting down to write a book
unless you feel that you must write that book, or else go
mad, or die." Robertson Davies (an interview?)

"Writers aren't people exactly...they're a whole lot of people
trying so hard to be one person." F. Scott Fitzgerald (The
Last Tycoon, 1941)

"Art is a lie that makes us realize truth." Pablo Picasso (The
Arts, Picasso Speaks, 1923)

www.ingramcontent.com/pod-product-compliance
Lightning Source LLC
Chambersburg PA
CBHW071321130626
46556CB00004B/1687